ESKIMO SONGS AND STORIES

ESKIMO

SONGS AND STORIES

collected by Knud Rasmussen
on the Fifth Thule Expedition

selected and translated by Edward Field

with illustrations by
KIAKSHUK AND PUDLO

A Merloyd Lawrence Book

DELACORTE PRESS / SEYMOUR LAWRENCE

The translations in this book were prepared originally as part of
Man: A Course of Study, a social science curriculum for
upper elementary grades developed by Education Development Center, Inc.,
under a grant from the National Science Foundation.

Illustrations and prints reproduced by permission of West Baffin Eskimo
Cooperative, Cape Dorset, N.W.T., Canada

Designed by Judith Lerner

Manufactured in the United States of America
Second Printing—1975

Library of Congress Cataloging in Publication Data

Field, Edward, 1924-
Eskimo songs and stories

SUMMARY: Poems based on songs and stories of the Netsilik Eskimos
reflect their daily life.
Retold from the literal English renderings in the official records
of Rasmussen's voyages published by the Royal Danish Archives.
Bibliography: p.
1. Eskimo poetry—Translations into English.
2. American poetry—Translations from Eskimo.
[1. Eskimo poetry—Translations into English.
2. American poetry—Translations from Eskimo]
I. Rasmussen, Knud Johan Victor, 1879-1933.
II. Kiakshuk, illus. III. Pudlo, illus. IV. Title.
PM64.Z95E5 1973 398.2'09701 73-3263

CONTENTS

ILLUSTRATIONS

KIAKSHUK

Eskimo Couple, Stonecut, 1961
Summer Camp Scene, Sealskin Stencil, 1961
Morning Sun, Sealskin Stencil, 1961
Three Bear Hunters, Sealskin Stencil, 1960
Seal Hunters, Sealskin Stencil, 1966
Seal Hunters on Sea Ice, Stonecut, 1961
Summer Caribou Hunt, Stonecut, 1960
Owl Attacking Snow Goose, Stonecut, 1961
Animal Spirit, Stonecut, 1966
Eskimo Wrestling Two Spirits, Sealskin Stencil, 1961
Eskimo Family Catching Fish, Sealskin Stencil, 1961

PUDLO

Thoughts of Walrus, Stonecut, 1961
Umingmuk (Musk Ox), Stonecut, 1970
Perils of the Hunter, Stonecut, 1970
Raven with Fish, Stonecut, 1963
Eagle Carrying Man, Stonecut, 1963

Man Carrying Reluctant Wife, Sealskin Stencil, 1961
Musk Ox Trappers, Stonecut, 1963
Man Carrying Bear, Sealskin Stencil, 1961
Spirits, Stonecut, 1966

ACKNOWLEDGMENTS

The publishers wish to thank Dorothy Eber of Montreal for thoughtful assistance in choosing and locating the original Eskimo prints which illustrate this book. Her advice, based upon extensive travel and research in the Arctic, was invaluable.

The Canadian Eskimo Arts Council and West Baffin Eskimo Cooperative graciously arranged for permission to reproduce the work of Kiakshuk and Pudlo. Alma Houston, executive secretary of the Council, was most helpful in making this possible.

Finally, the publishers wish to thank the National Museum of Man in Ottawa for kind permission to reproduce works by Kiakshuk and Pudlo in its collection.

INTRODUCTION

These poems are based on songs and stories collected by the famous Danish explorer Knud Rasmussen. During the expedition he led across arctic America, known as the Fifth Thule Expedition, Rasmussen lived for some time with the Netsilik Eskimos, a remote tribe who live along the coast above the Arctic Circle. It was among these isolated people "cut off from the surrounding world by ice-filled seas and enormous trackless wastes" that Rasmussen recorded the legends and tales collected here. The poet Edward Field has selected and retold the best of them.

Knud Rasmussen, who was part Eskimo and spent his boyhood in Greenland, spoke the Eskimo language. This language is similar all the way from Greenland across the North American continent to Alaska. During his years of travel in the Arctic, Rasmussen found that the ancient stories were the same from tribe to tribe, even though these people lived thousands of miles apart. The fears and beliefs and joys expressed in these songs and stories are those of all Eskimos.

The Netsilik, who call themselves the "people of the seal," were sought out by Rasmussen because they were more remote than other tribes, and in those days (1921–1924) completely untouched by modern technology. They live in one of the bleakest and most forbidding parts of the world, where winter lasts for ten months, where the temperature drops to 50 degrees below zero, where there are no trees, where the ocean freezes solid for seven months. By sharing the rugged life of this one tribe, Rasmussen felt that he could learn a great deal about the ways of all Eskimos. He not only studied how they lived, how they fished at their stone weirs, how they hunted seal and caribou or built their igloos, he also wanted to know what they believed and feared and how they understood the universe. For in their struggle to survive in a land which seems to be no more than a frozen desert, the Eskimos developed their own way of looking at the world. To see the world through Eskimo eyes, Knud Rasmussen listened carefully to the stories and their magic incantations or songs. By reading these collected here, we too can understand Eskimo ideas of life and death, of the forces which control the world and which brought it into being.

An Eskimo named Orpingalik, who was admired by his tribe as a singer and poet, once explained to Rasmussen what a song meant to him and how a new song comes to be. Rasmussen recorded this explanation in his book *The Netsilik Eskimos:* "Songs are thoughts, sung out with the breath when people are moved by great forces and ordinary speech no longer suffices.

"Man is moved just like the ice floe sailing here and there out in the current. His thoughts are driven by a flowing force when he feels joy, when he feels fear, when he feels sorrow. Thoughts can wash over him like a flood, making breath come in gasps and his heart throb.... It will happen that we, who always think we are small, will feel still smaller. And we will fear to use words. But it will happen that the words we need will come of themselves. When the words we want to use shoot up of themselves... we get a new song."

ESKIMO SONGS AND STORIES

SONGS MY MOTHER TAUGHT ME

I am just an ordinary woman
who has never had visions.
But I will tell you what I can
about this world I know
and about the other worlds I do not know personally.
I don't even dream at night—
if I did I would know more than I do.
People who dream
hear and see many important things. In sleep
people can live a completely different life
from real life.

I believe in dreams
but not being a dreamer myself
I only know what every child learns from his mother,
for mothers tell children stories at bedtime
to put them to sleep
and it is from these stories
we learn about things.

I have never forgotten the old tales
I heard from my mother.
I have told them to my children and grandchildren,
and I will tell them to you.

KIAKSHUK / *Eskimo Couple*

THE EARTH AND THE PEOPLE

The earth was here before the people.
The very first people
came out of the ground.
Everything came from the ground,
even caribou.
Children once grew
out of the ground
just as flowers do.
Women out wandering
found them sprawling on the grass
and took them home and nursed them.
That way people multiplied.

This land of ours
has become habitable
because we came here
and learned how to hunt.

KIAKSHUK / *Summer Camp Scene*

Even so, up here where we live
life is one continuous fight
for food and for clothing
and a struggle against bad hunting
and snow storms and sickness.

But we know our land is not the whole world.

MAGIC WORDS

In the very earliest time,
when both people and animals lived on earth,
a person could become an animal if he wanted to
and an animal could become a human being.
Sometimes they were people
and sometimes animals
and there was no difference.
All spoke the same language.

That was the time when words were like magic.
The human mind had mysterious powers.
A word spoken by chance
might have strange consequences.
It would suddenly come alive
and what people wanted to happen could happen.
All you had to do was say it.
Nobody could explain this,
that's the way it was.

PUDLO / *Thoughts of Walrus*

DAY AND NIGHT:
HOW THEY CAME TO BE

In those times
when just saying a word
could make something happen,
there was no light on earth yet.
Everything was in darkness all the time,
people lived in darkness.

A fox and a hare had an argument,
each saying his magic word:
"Darkness," said the fox,
for he wanted it to be dark so he could go hunting.

"Day," said the hare,
for he wanted daylight
so he could find good grass to eat.

The hare won: His word was more powerful
and he got his wish:
Day came, replacing night.
But the word of the fox was powerful too
and when day was over, night came,
and from then on they took turns with each other,
the nighttime of the fox
following the daytime of the hare.

THE THINGS IN THE SKY

The weather with its storms and snows
was once an orphan child
who was so cruelly treated, as orphans often are,
that he went up into the sky to take revenge.
That's where the bad weather came from
that ruins hunting and brings hunger.

The stars too are people
who suddenly raised themselves from the earth
and were fixed in the sky.
Some hunters were out chasing a bear
when they all rose up in the air
and became a group of stars.
Every constellation has such a story.

The northern lights are a celestial ball game:
They flicker over the sky
like a ball being kicked around
by players running on a field.

The rainbow is the shape of a great doorway,
opening, perhaps, to some world we still do not know.
But it is so far away
that no one has to be afraid
of the lovely-colored light in the sky.

SUN AND MOON

A brother and sister had been very wicked.
They were so ashamed of themselves
they decided to change into something else
and start over in a new life.

The sister cried out of her unhappiness:
"Brother, what shall we turn into? Wolves?"

Her brother, not as anxious as she was to change, replied:
"Not wolves, sister, their teeth are so sharp."

"Brother, shall we be bears?" she asked desperately.
"Not bears, sister, they are too clumsy," he answered, hoping she would accept his excuse.

"Brother, what in the world shall we be? Musk oxen?"
"Not musk oxen, their horns are too sharp."

"Brother, shall we be seals then?"
"No, sister, they have sharp claws."

And in this way they discussed all the animals and the brother succeeded in vetoing all of them.

At last his sister moaned, "Brother,
shall we become the Sun and the Moon?"

Her brother really could think of no objection to that,
hard as he tried,
so they each lighted a torch of moss from the fire
and holding the flames high
they ran out of their snow hut.

They ran round and round it,
the brother chasing his sister faster and faster,
until they took off into the air.
They rose and rose and kept on rising
right up into the sky.
But as they went, the sister put out her brother's torch
because he had been reluctant.

She with her lighted torch became the Sun
and now warms the whole earth,
but her brother, the Moon, is cold
because his torch no longer burns.

KIAKSHUK / *Morning Sun*

THUNDER AND LIGHTNING

Once in a time of hunger
the people were on the move
looking for better hunting grounds.
Coming to a wide rushing river
the men made a ferry out of the kayaks
by tying them together with thongs
and brought the women and children across.

There were two orphans
whom nobody would bother about:
In the hungry times people only had enough
for their own children.
So no one took them
and they were left behind on the shore.

They stood there, the little boy and little girl,
watching the people go off without them.
How would they live? They had nothing to eat
and did not know how to take care of themselves.

They wandered back to the old campsite
to look for something to eat.
The girl only found a piece of flint,
and the boy, an old leather boot sole.

The boy said to his sister,
"After the way we have been treated
I can't bear to be a human being any longer.
What can we turn into?"
"Caribou?" his sister suggested,
thinking of the warm herds and the moss to eat.
"No," he answered, "for then men would spear us to death."
"Seals?" she asked.
"No, for then they would tear us to pieces for food."

And in this way they named all the creatures
but there wasn't one
that wasn't a victim of man.

Finally the sister proposed turning into thunder and lightning.
"That's it!" said her brother,
and they became airy spirits and rose into the sky,
the girl striking sparks with her flint
and the boy banging his piece of leather like a drum
making the heavens flash and thunder.

They soon revenged themselves
on the people who left them to starve.
They made so much thunder and lightning over their camp
that everyone died of fright.
And that way people discovered
that thunder and lightning could be very dangerous indeed.

HOW WE KNOW ABOUT ANIMALS

There was once a wise man
who turned himself into all the different kinds of animals
to see what it was like to be them.

That happened long ago in the old times
when there was not much difference yet
between an animal's soul and a human's
so to change from one creature into another
was not too hard, if you knew how.
And this man knew the trick.

First he tried being a bear
but that was a tiring life, they walk about so much.
Even at night they keep roaming, the furry wanderers.

When he had enough of that, he became a seal:
They are always playing in the water
making the waves go to and fro.
Seals like sports
and turn themselves into people sometimes for fun
and shoot at targets of snow, like we do,
with bows and arrows.

Then the wise man turned into a wolf
but that was a hard life and he nearly starved
until another wolf showed him
how to get a good grip on the ground with his claws
and run with the pack.
That way he learned how to keep up with the others
and bring down caribou.

Then he became a musk ox:
How warm it was in the middle of the big lowing herds
huddled together.

PUDLO / *Musk Ox*

And after that he became a caribou, strange beasts,
so timid that out of a sound sleep
they would jump up and gallop away
scared by a nothing.
How unpleasant to be a caribou!

That is how the wise man
lived the lives of all the animals.
He learned their secrets
and taught us all we know about them.

HISTORY OF THE TUNRIT

When our forefathers came to these hunting grounds
the Tunrit people already lived here.
It was the Tunrit who first learned
how to survive in this difficult country.
They showed us the caribou crossing places
and taught us the special way to fish in the rivers.

Our people came from inland
so we love caribou hunting more than anything else,
but the Tunrit were sea people
and preferred to hunt seal.
They actually went out on the salt sea in their kayaks,
hunting seal in open water. That takes nerve.
We only hunt them through the ice at their breathing holes.
They also caught whales and walruses as they swam by:
The bones of these creatures are still lying around
in the wrecks of the Tunrit houses.
And they hunted bear and wore their skins for clothes.
We wear caribou.

The Tunrit were strong, but easily frightened.
In a fight they would rather run than kill. Anyway,
you never heard of them killing anyone.

And we lived among the Tunrit in those days peacefully,
for they let us come and share their land:
Until once by accident some of them killed one of our dogs
and ran away scared, leaving their homeland.

PUDLO / *Perils of the Hunter*

All of the Tunrit fled from their villages here finally,
although we cannot remember why anymore:
They just ran away or the land was taken from them.
And on leaving us they cried:
"We followed the caribou and hunted them down,
now it is your turn to follow them and do the hunting."

And so we do to this day.

THE LAZY TUNRIT

This is the story of the Tunrit man
who was too lazy to hunt caribou.
(Tunrit, you know, prefer hunting seal.)
His job in the caribou hunt
was to go out on the land
and scare up animals down to the crossing place
where the kayaks waited.
But this one was a tired Tunrit
and he lay down to rest
and spent the rest of the day resting.
He didn't want to admit he had done this
so he rubbed his boot-soles against a rough stone.
And when he came home that night
he said, "What a day hunting caribou!"
and showed his worn-out soles
to prove how far he had gone.
So this way he used to rest all day
and go home only at evening in time for dinner and sleep.
His wife was kept busy making him new soles.
"My man," she thought, "what a walker!"

But meanwhile few caribou were coming to the crossing place
so the hunters waiting there
decided to spy on him.
They followed him and saw him lie down
and rub his soles against a big white stone—
lying down walking, he rubbed his soles to and fro
until there were holes in them
and when evening came they saw the walker
limp home to his tent exhausted.
So they found him out
and named this stone The Sole-Wearer-Outer.
That famous sole-wearing stone still exists in our land
and is still used, they say,
by some of our biggest walkers.

THE GIANT BEAR

There once was a giant bear
who followed people for his prey.
He was so big he swallowed them whole:
Then they smothered to death inside him
if they hadn't already died of fright.

Either the bear attacked them on the run,
or if they crawled into a cave
where he could not squeeze his enormous body in,
he stabbed them with his whiskers like toothpicks,
drawing them out one by one,
and gulped them down.

No one knew what to do
until a wise man went out and let the bear swallow him,
sliding right down his throat into the big, dark, hot, slimy stomach.
And once inside there, he took his knife
and simply cut him open,
killing him of course.

He carved a door in the bear's belly
and threw out those who had been eaten before,
and then he stepped out himself
and went home to get help with the butchering.

Everyone lived on bear meat for a long time.
That's the way it goes:
Monster one minute, food the next.

KIAKSHUK / *Three Bear Hunters*

AN ESKIMO TAUNTS HIS RIVAL IN SINGING AND HUNTING

I know you, my friend. The way you talk
one would think you never lost a race.
Well, I dare you: The next time
a caribou with a rack of great antlers
swims across that lake over there
and the weather is so cold the kayaks ice up
making them really hard to paddle,
let's chase it then,
I mean let's just the two of us race
with our wives watching from the shore:
Who do you think will come in last?
I'll tell you who: Remember that time
long ago when the two of us were young
and the kayaks went like a pack of wolves
after a caribou out on the big lake there?

I clearly remember you couldn't paddle nearly fast enough
but trailed well behind—
behind ME, my friend.
And you expect me to sing your praises now?

THE FLY AND
THE WATER BEETLE

A fly and a water bug
were having a fight.
The fly razzed the bug,
"Beetle, you've got no guts
or you'd answer me good."

And the beetle said,
"I may not have guts like you
but just wait, I'll give you a sharp reply."
And making as fierce a face as he could
the bug turned his back on the wise-guy fly.

But he didn't make the slightest attempt to answer him
for he was not good at thinking up answers.

THE RAVEN AND THE GULL HAVE A SPAT

RAVEN: You dirty-white slob of a gull,
what are you plumping yourself down around here for?
You're no match for me
so better not start anything, big boy.

PUDLO / *Raven with Fish*

GULL: Who's trying to tell me what I can't do?
When the streams run free of ice in spring
who goes spear-fishing with his beak? ME!
That's something you can't do, short bill,
and never will.

RAVEN: Oh yeah? But when it's freezing out
you have to stay home, crying from hunger.
You're pecking bones while I'm eating berries.
So what did you say I couldn't do?

TOTANGUAK,
SPIRIT OF STRING FIGURES

One night when everyone was sleeping
a child lay awake making string figures to amuse himself
and a stranger appeared before him out of the night.

"I dare you," he said to the child,
"let us see who can make string figures faster.
I set the rules: We will make three of them,
the first two you may choose,
and if you win those you may also choose the last one.
But if I win the first two
then I get to choose the last."

The foolish child agreed to this
for he was very proud of his skill at string figures,
and for the first test chose *The Spouting Whale,*
but as fast as his fingers went, the stranger was faster
and finished before him.

Then he proposed *Man Carrying Kayak* for the second race,
his best string figure,
but the stranger's fingers flew like the wind
and beat him again.

"So," said the stranger with a frightening hiss,
"you have lost the first two.
Now it is my turn to choose the last,
and I propose the string figure of *Totanguak!"*

Then the child knew who this strange opponent was,
none other than Totanguak himself, Spirit of String Figures,
and if he lost this final race he would be carried off
and never see his people again.

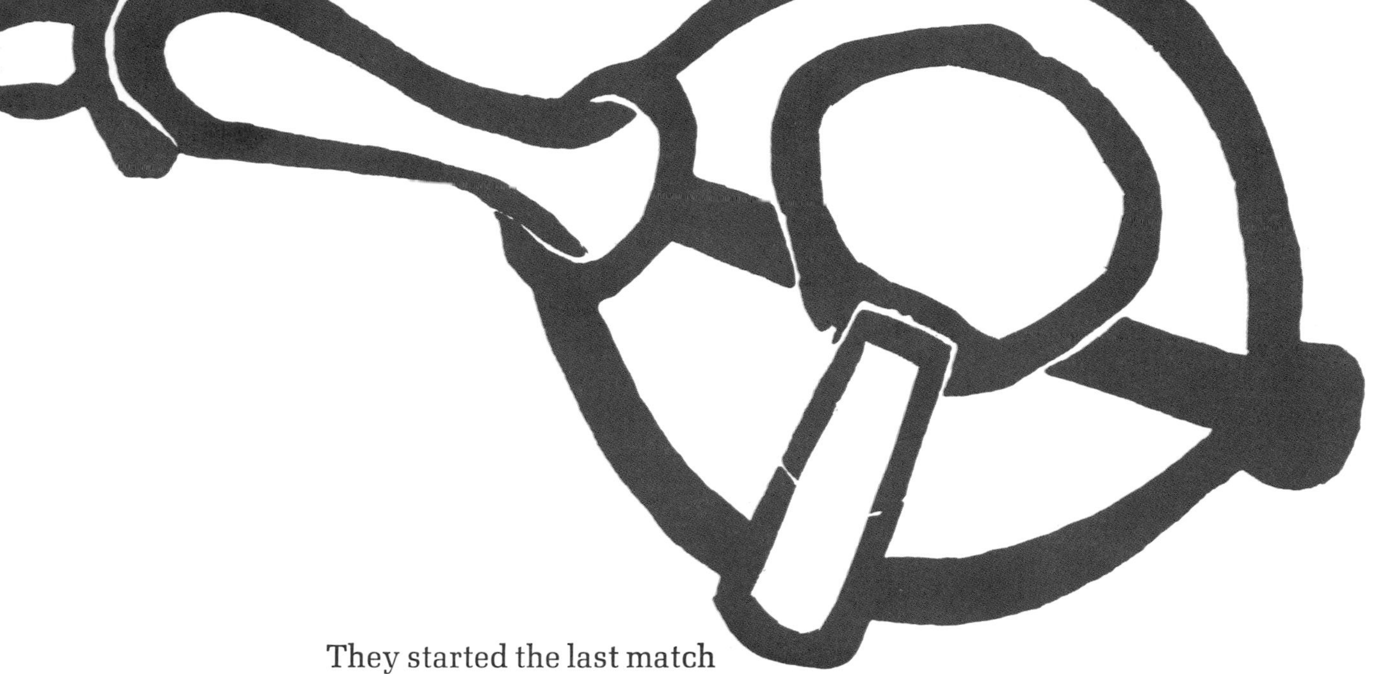

They started the last match
and the child simply stopped and watched the gruesome sight
as Totanguak running out of string used his own intestines
to create the complicated figure.

Totanguak gave a cry of triumph as he finished
and the child knew he was doomed—Totanguak would get him now!
But at that moment his father on the sleeping platform near him
woke up and raised his head
and Totanguak vanished into the air with a hiss!

That is why children are forbidden
to play at string figures by themselves at night.

A PEEK INTO AN OWL'S HOUSE, OR JUST LIKE HUMANS

BIG POPPA OWL: Our two sons ought to be back soon from hunting.
Keep a look out, Momma,
and see if they come back with anything to eat.

BIG MOMMA OWL: There they come, our darlings,
each dragging a marmot!

BIG POPPA OWL: Yum, yum, I can't wait.
I'll go help them.
I'd better hitch up the sled.
Where's the dog harness?

BIG MOMMA OWL: Over by the door,
but I'm afraid the breast strap is still broken.
I meant to mend it but just plain forgot.

BIG POPPA OWL: (hollering)
What do you mean forgot?
You didn't have a thing to do all day.

BIG MOMMA OWL: (crying)
But the baby was so cranky today,
he took up all my time.

They were really going at it
by the time the two sons came home
each dragging a marmot
and found their parents squabbling,
the baby crying, and the pot boiling over.

MAGIC WORDS
TO FEEL BETTER

SEA GULL
who flaps his wings
over my head
            in the blue air,

you GULL up there
dive down
          come here
take me with you
              in the air!

Wings flash by
my mind's eye
and I'm up there sailing
in the cool air,
            a-a-a-a-a-ah,
                        in the air.

PUDLO / *Eagle Carrying Man*

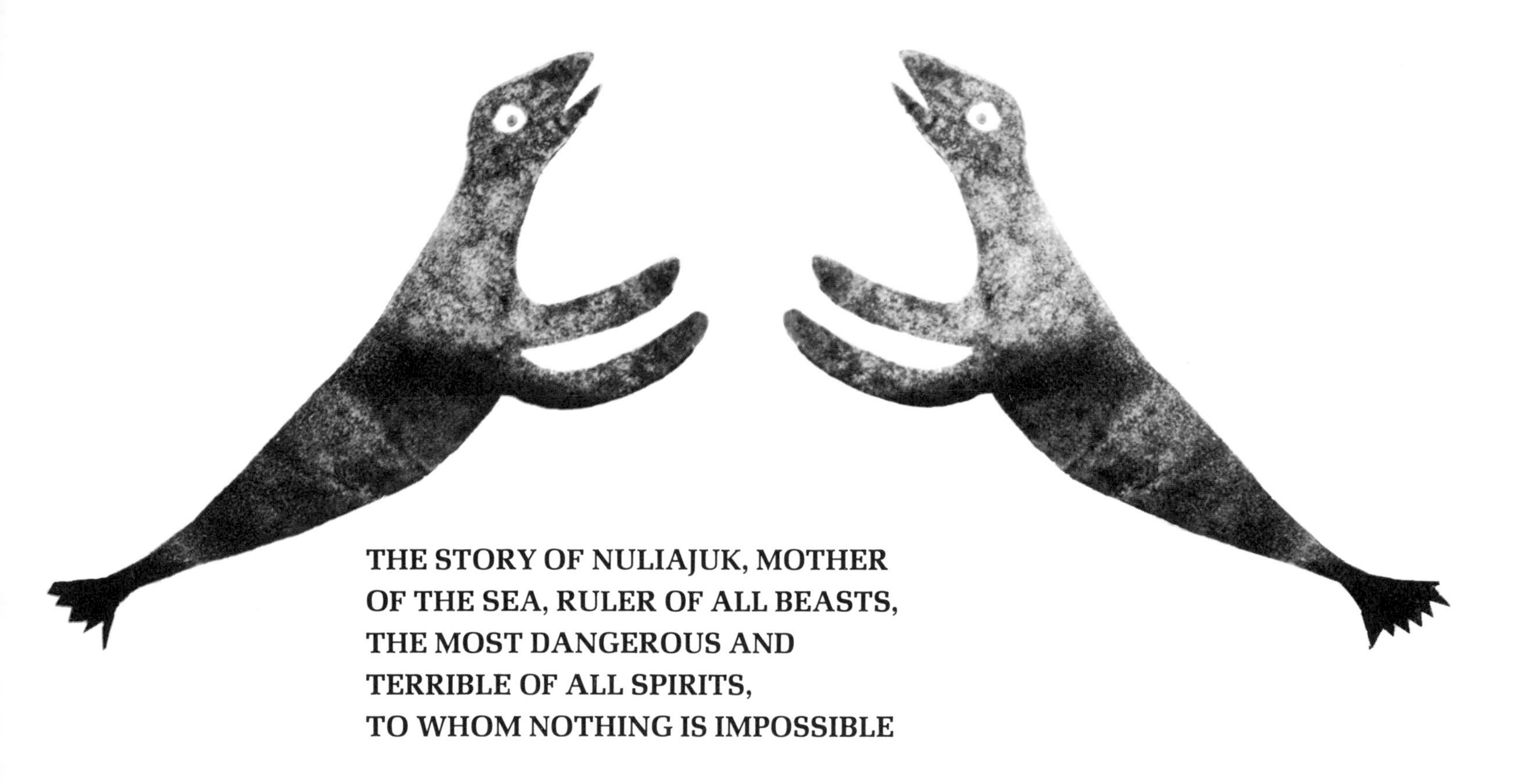

THE STORY OF NULIAJUK, MOTHER OF THE SEA, RULER OF ALL BEASTS, THE MOST DANGEROUS AND TERRIBLE OF ALL SPIRITS, TO WHOM NOTHING IS IMPOSSIBLE

In a time of famine once
when the whole village was going off to new hunting grounds
a little orphan girl named Nuliajuk
was left behind. Nobody could bother
about an extra mouth to feed.

They were in a hurry
to get to a place where there was food.
They made a raft of the kayaks to cross the river on
and the parents put their children on board.
Little Nuliajuk who had no one to take care of her
jumped out on the raft as it left the shore
wanting to go too,
but the people threw her off into the water.

The little girl tried to hold on to the edge of the raft
but they cut her fingers off
and as she went under
the pieces of her fingers came alive in the water
and turned into seals:
That's where seals came from.

And Nuliajuk floated to the bottom
where she became Mother of the Sea
and Ruler of All Beasts on sea and land.

There she lives in her house under the waters
and keeps track of everything we do,
and when we break taboos she punishes us
by hiding the animals. Then hunting is bad
and people starve. That is why
she is the most feared of all the gods.

Nuliajuk gave seals to mankind, it is true,
but she is not friendly to people
for they had no pity on her when she lived on earth,
throwing her into the sea like that to drown.
So naturally she would like mankind to perish too.
That is why we do our best
to be as good as we can
and make Nuliajuk think kindly of us.

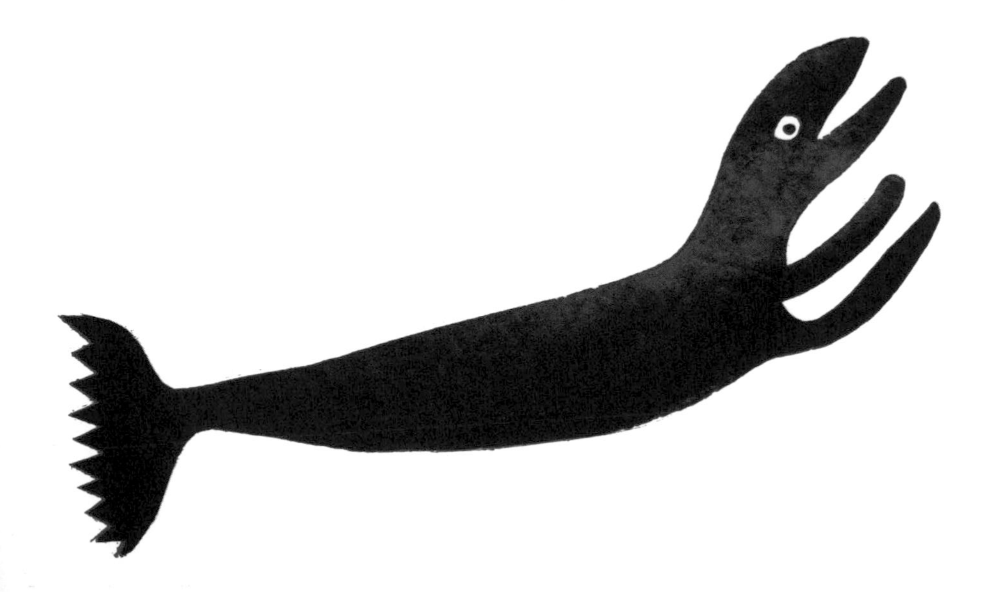

PRAYER FOR GOOD SEAL HUNTING

O sea goddess Nuliajuk,
when you were a little unwanted orphan girl
we let you drown.
You fell in the water
and when you hung onto the kayaks crying
we cut off your fingers.
So you sank into the sea
and your fingers turned into
the innumerable seals.

You sweet orphan Nuliajuk,
I beg you now
bring me a gift,
not anything from the land
but a gift from the sea,
something that will make a nice soup.
Dare I say it right out?
I want a seal!

You dear little orphan,
creep out of the water
panting on this beautiful shore,
puh, puh, like this, puh, puh,
O welcome gift
in the shape of a seal!

KIAKSHUK / *Seal Hunters*

NETSERSUITSUARSUK

This unpronounceable name
was the name of a man who could never catch a seal:
Net-ser su-it su-ar-suk.

When the men came home from hunting at the breathing holes
and his wife saw her neighbor's husband
drag a fat seal into the igloo next door
and her own husband came in with nothing
she was furious.
So when he asked her for a drink of water
she wouldn't give him a drop.

Every day it was like this: He came home,
this hunter with permanent hard luck,
and asked his wife for a drink,
and every time she refused him.
What quarrels they had, until one day he said,
"I'm fed up. No water? No husband!"
And he went out for a walk and didn't come back.

When night came he arrived at a house
where three bears lived
and when he told them his troubles
they kindly invited him to stay with them.
He did, until one day he found that he missed his wife
and went home again.

The first thing he said when he came in the door was
"Am I thirsty! How about a drink?"

His wife answered as usual,
"Still no seal? Then no water
for Net-ser su-it su-ar-suk!"

At this, he stared hard at the bearskin on the sleeping platform
sending a mental message to the bears for help.
Right away the snow outside began to crunch
with heavy footfalls of a bear:
It was a new helping spirit that his friends had sent,
and a great paw smashed the ice-window of the igloo.
The wife immediately understood that things had changed
and cried, "Here is water, darling Net-ser su-it su-ar-suk!"
And the bear vanished.

From then on, Net-ser su-it su-ar-suk
had a good little willing wife
who did everything he wanted:
He only had to glance at the bearskin to make her jump!
And even his luck at the breathing holes changed—
now he caught many seals
and was known as
The Mighty Hunter Net-ser su-it su-ar-suk!

TRAVEL SONG

Leaving the white bear behind in his realm of sea ice
we set off for our winter hunting grounds on the inland bays.
This is the route we took:
First we made our way across dangerous Dead-man's Gulch
and then crossed High-in-the-sky Mountain.
Circling Crooked Lake
we followed the course of the river over the flatlands beyond
where the sleds sank in deep snow up to the cross slats.
It was sweaty work, I tell you,
helping the dogs.

You think I even had a small fish
or a piece of musk ox meat to chew on?
Don't make me laugh: I didn't have a shred on me.
The journey went on and on.
It was exhausting pushing the sled along the lakes
around one island and over another,
pushing, pushing.

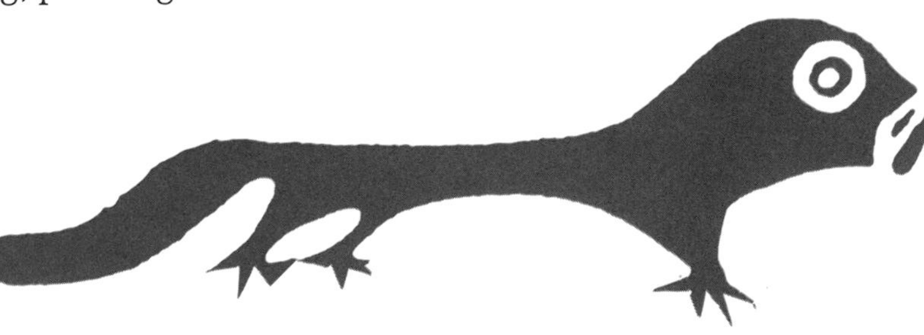

When we passed the island called Big Pot
we spit at it
just to do something different for a change.

Then after Stony Island
we crossed over Water Sound at the narrows,
touching on the two islands like crooked eyes
that we call, naturally, Cross-Eyed Islands,
and arrived at Seal Bay, where we camped,

KIAKSHUK / *Seal Hunters on Sea Ice*

and settled down to a winter season
of hunting at the breathing holes
for the delicious small blubber beasts.

Such is our life,
the life of hunters
migrating with the season.

GRANDMA TAKES A FOSTER CHILD

Grandma turned a little odd in spring:
She took a caterpillar in and mothered it.
She put it down her sleeve
while she went about her work,
letting it suck like a baby on her skin,
and soon it grew so big and fat and happy
it said, Jeetsee-jeetsee.

Her grandchildren saw this and were disgusted—
after all, a caterpillar!
So when grandma went behind the tent to pee,
they threw it to the sled-dogs
who gobbled the juicy tidbit up.

And when grandma came back in
she called, My darling? My own one?
Why don't I hear the song that made my old heart young again?
Where is my dear one that went Jeetsee?
Gone?
And she sat down crying by the fire alone.

MAGIC WORDS
FOR HUNTING CARIBOU

You, you, caribou
yes you
        long legs
yes you
        long ears
you with the long neck hair—
From far off you're little as a louse:
Be my swan, fly to me, long horns waving
big bull
        cari-bou-bou-bou.
Put your footprints on this land—
this land I'm standing on
is rich with the lichens you love.
See, I'm holding in my hand
the reindeer moss you're dreaming of—
so delicious, yum, yum, yum—
Come, caribou, come.

Come on, move them bones,
move your leg bones back and forth
and give yourself to me.
I'm here,
I'm waiting
                just for YOU
you, you, caribou.
Appear!
COME HERE!

KIAKSHUK / *Summer Caribou Hunt*

ANNINGAT

An old woman had a dog she named Anningat
after her daughter who was living
far away in another village.
Everybody laughed.
How can you name a dog after your daughter? they asked.

Okay, laugh, she answered,
but every time I feed my dog
I make believe I am feeding my darling daughter,
for how do I know she isn't hungry
far away from her momma?
This way I feel like I am feeding her every day.
And when I call my dog by my daughter's name
it's just as if my daughter whom I love was near.
If I always keep my dog Anningat with me,
name will call to name
and Anningat, my daughter, will often come to visit.

THE WOMAN WHO TURNED TO STONE

A woman once refused to get married
and turned down every man who proposed to her,
so finally one of them said:
"You've got a heart of stone
and I hope you turn into stone!"

And before she could answer with her famous sharp tongue
his words began to come true
and she could no longer move
from the spot where she was standing by the lake.
She was really turning into stone from the legs up.
Desperately she called to some kayaks paddling by:
"Kayaks, please come here boys,
I'm ready to get married now."
(Now she was willing to marry not just one
but as many as she could get!)
But the men wouldn't come near her
having been rejected too often.
She clapped her hands and sang her song:
"Kayaks everywhere,
please come here,
I'll take you all as husbands now.
Men, have pity on me
before my precious hands
have turned to stone."
But then her hands turned to stone,
stone was her tongue,
and her song was done.

That stone is still there by the lake shore.
It doesn't look like a person anymore.
Hardly any of it shows now
because people have heaped it over
with small white stones as offerings to her spirit.
For it is said that since turning to stone
she likes to have possessions of stone,
and people think that if they give her what she wants
she will give them good hunting.

PUDLO / *Man Carrying Reluctant Wife*

COURTING SONG

The Owl saw the Plover crying and asked,
"Why are you crying, my pretty bird?"

"My husband, my poor husband," the Plover sobbed.
"A man caught him in a snare, and I have lost him."

"Well," said the Owl, "then why don't you take me,
handsome me, for your next husband,
with my bushy eyebrows and long beard,
my plump feathers and lofty forehead?"

"Huh," said the Plover, "who would have you, I wonder,
even with your plump feathers and long beard,
your lofty forehead and bushy eyebrows?
Look at you, you have no neck and stubby legs!"

The Owl hollered back, "You dirty bird,
so you won't have me for a husband?
Then I hope you end up a tidbit between someone's teeth!"

KIAKSHUK / *Owl Attacking Snow Goose*

THE DEATH OF KIGTAK

One bad winter when everyone was weak with hunger
and the village decided to move to new hunting grounds,
Arfek had to leave behind his old mother-in-law Kigtak
to crawl over the ice and catch up if she could.
It was a pitiful sight and we did not laugh
for it probably meant death for her:
The old lady was half-blind and crippled
and she was not wearing warm enough clothes for the weather
but as long as she could crawl she followed:
Life was still sweet to her.

No one here among us wishes harm to old people
for we ourselves might live to be old some day,
but Arfek had no choice but to leave Old Kigtak behind.
He couldn't let her ride on the sledge,
for he had only two dogs, and as it was
he and his wife had to help drag the sledge, weak as they were.

He couldn't go back to get her after they camped
because that would mean spending the night
traveling back and forth
when he had to be at the breathing holes
early next morning to hunt for food.
He could not allow his wife and children to starve:
He had to think of them first
for they had their lives ahead of them,
rather than help an old worn-out woman
who was at death's door anyway.

We have a custom that old people who cannot work anymore
should help death to take them.
Old Kigtak thought of this, left behind, all alone on the ice.
She knew she was useless and couldn't work anymore,
so why hang on as a burden to her children?

You see, it is not that we have hard hearts
but that the conditions of life here are merciless
and to survive in a land of ice and snow
sometimes we must be without pity.

THE EVIL SPIRIT
AND THE BEARDED SEAL

Some children were playing and laughing as they do,
when an evil spirit got sick of hearing them so happy
and grabbed a live bearded seal for a whip to beat them with
and went after them.

When they saw him with that big weapon in his hand
and heard his awful threats
they climbed up on a tall snow-block used for stretching skins
where he could not get them.

Foiled, he got madder than ever
and decided to break into the snow house
used as a community center,
and he crawled in through the long low entrance passage
pushing his seal before him.

KIAKSHUK / *Animal Spirit*

Right inside the inner door-flap
there were people boiling blubber
and when the spirit's horrible face came into view
they poured the pot of boiling oil right over him,
scalding him to death.
The seal that he used to beat people with
was flopping around on the floor
so they made short work of him too:
They put him out of his misery fast with a knife—
into the blubber pot with him and that was that!

THE INVISIBLE MEN

There is a tribe of invisible men
who move around us like shadows—have you felt them?
They have bodies like ours and live like us,
using the same kind of weapons and tools.
You can see their tracks in the snow sometimes
and even their snow houses
but never the invisible men themselves.
They cannot be seen until they die—
then they become visible.

It once happened that a human woman
married one of the invisible men.
He was a good husband in every way:
He went out hunting and brought her food,
and they could talk together like any other couple.
But the wife could not bear the thought
that she did not know what the man she married looked like.

One day when they were both at home
she was so overcome with curiosity to see him
that she stabbed with a knife where she knew he was sitting.
And her desire was fulfilled:
Before her eyes a handsome young man fell to the floor.
But he was cold and dead, and too late
she realized what she had done,
and sobbed her heart out.

When the invisible men heard about this murder
they came out of their snow huts to take revenge.
Their bows were seen moving through the air
and the bow strings stretching as they aimed their arrows.
The humans stood there helplessly
for they had no idea what to do or how to fight
because they could not see their assailants.
But the invisible men had a code of honor
that forbade them to attack opponents
who could not defend themselves,
so they did not let their arrows fly,
and nothing happened. There was no battle after all
and everyone went back to their ordinary lives.

LAZY ESKIMO

When I go out for caribou cow
I get myself a caribou cow.
But my friend, some hunter he is:
he's lazy as a dog. Big shot,
he's lying in the igloo dreaming of big game.

Friend, you'd better practice on caribou
before you go out on the ice
and face the claws and jaws of the white bear
or the horns of the black musk ox charging you,
poor you and your little spear.

PUDLO / *Musk Ox Trappers*

A LESSON IN SHARING

A lame man asked Kaluarsuk to move in with him
and be his hunting mate.
This lame man wasn't able to walk
but he was good at paddling a kayak
so Kaluarsuk teamed up with him
and during the caribou season they shared the meat.

But when winter came, Kaluarsuk figured
that the lame one was not good for much
when it came to hunting at the breathing holes.
He couldn't get there over the ice with his bad legs, could he?
So when Kaluarsuk went out and caught seal
he did not share any with his lame buddy at home
and never gave him a bite to eat.

KIAKSHUK / *Eskimo Family Catching Fish*

Two brothers next door saw the poor cripple dying of hunger
and took pity on him
and brought him into their house
telling their wives to feed him dried salmon to revive him.
And when the lame man was no longer weak from hunger
they took him with them to the breathing holes
by driving him there on a sled
and he turned out to be a good shot with a harpoon.
In fact he caught seals right away
which he shared with his old sharing partner,
Kaluarsuk, who had come along.

Kaluarsuk who had caught nothing himself that day
took his share of seal
and said, "How good to have hunting companion."
The two brothers spoke right up:
"You like having hunting mates now?
Then why didn't you think of your hunting mate
when you were the one catching seals!"

ORPINGALIK'S SONG:
IN A TIME OF SICKNESS

My biggest worry is this:
that the whole winter
I have been sick and helpless as a child.
  Poor me.

As long as I'm in this condition
I really think it would be better
if my wife left me
for I'm not much of a husband anymore.
I should be taking care of her and getting food.
What good am I
now that I can't get up on my feet?

Have you forgotten what a man you were? I ask myself.
Try to remember the beasts you hunted.
Remember and be strong again.

Yes, I remember once coming on a great white bear
who thought he alone was a fighter.
What a battle we had!
He came straight at me across the ice
rising high on his hind legs.
We grappled, and again and again
he threw me down,
but I didn't let go until he was dead.
When the bear came out of the water that day
and lay down calmly on the ice
he thought he was the only male around
but I came along and showed him!

I also remember a seal I once got
in a time when we were all weak with hunger.
Everyone was still asleep
when I went out on the ice that morning
and luckily found the breathing hole of a seal.
That blubbery beast was in there all right
about to come up for a breath of air
but he heard me, the sly one,
and waited to one side under the thick ice
where I could not spear him through the hole.
But just as I was ready to give up
he made a false move and I got my harpoon into him,
and we had his blubber and blood for breakfast that day!

Now with me sick
there is no blubber in the house
to fill the lamp with.
Spring has come
and the good days for hunting
are passing, one by one.
When shall I get well?
My wife has to go begging
skins for clothes and meat to eat
that I can't provide.
O when shall I be well again?

I can't understand it:
I was once a hunter
but now I've come to this.
What a hunter I was.

I remember a fat caribou cow
swimming out in the open water,
and I went after her in my kayak
hardly believing I could ever catch up.

PUDLO / *Man Carrying Bear*

I chased hard
—I almost feel strong again remembering it—
and other kayaks were chasing too
thinking they would get the caribou first.
They were already shouting cries of victory
but I put everything I had into my paddle,
—O I remember now how it feels to be a real man again—
and I won the race:
It was my caribou, all mine,
and the others got nothing at all!

HUNGER

You, stranger, who only see us happy and free of care,
if you knew the horrors we often have to live through
you would understand our love of eating and singing and dancing.
There is not one among us
who hasn't lived through a winter of bad hunting
when many people starved to death.
We are never surprised to hear
that someone has died of starvation—we are used to it.
And they are not to blame: Sickness comes,
or bad weather ruins hunting,
as when a blizzard of snow hides the breathing holes of the seals.

I once saw a wise old man hang himself
because he was starving to death
and preferred to die in his own way.
But before he died he filled his mouth with seal bones,
for that way he was sure to get plenty of meat
in the Land of the Dead.

Once during the winter famine
a woman gave birth to a child
while people lay round about her dying of hunger.
What could the baby want with life here on earth?
And how could it live when its mother herself
was dried up with starvation?
So she strangled it and let it freeze.
And later on ate it to keep alive.
Then a seal was caught and the famine was over,
so the mother survived.
But from that time on she was paralyzed
because she had eaten part of herself.

That is what can happen to people.
We have gone through it ourselves
and know what one may come to, so we do not judge them.
And how would anyone who has eaten his fill and is well
be able to understand the madness of hunger?
We only know that we all want so much to live!

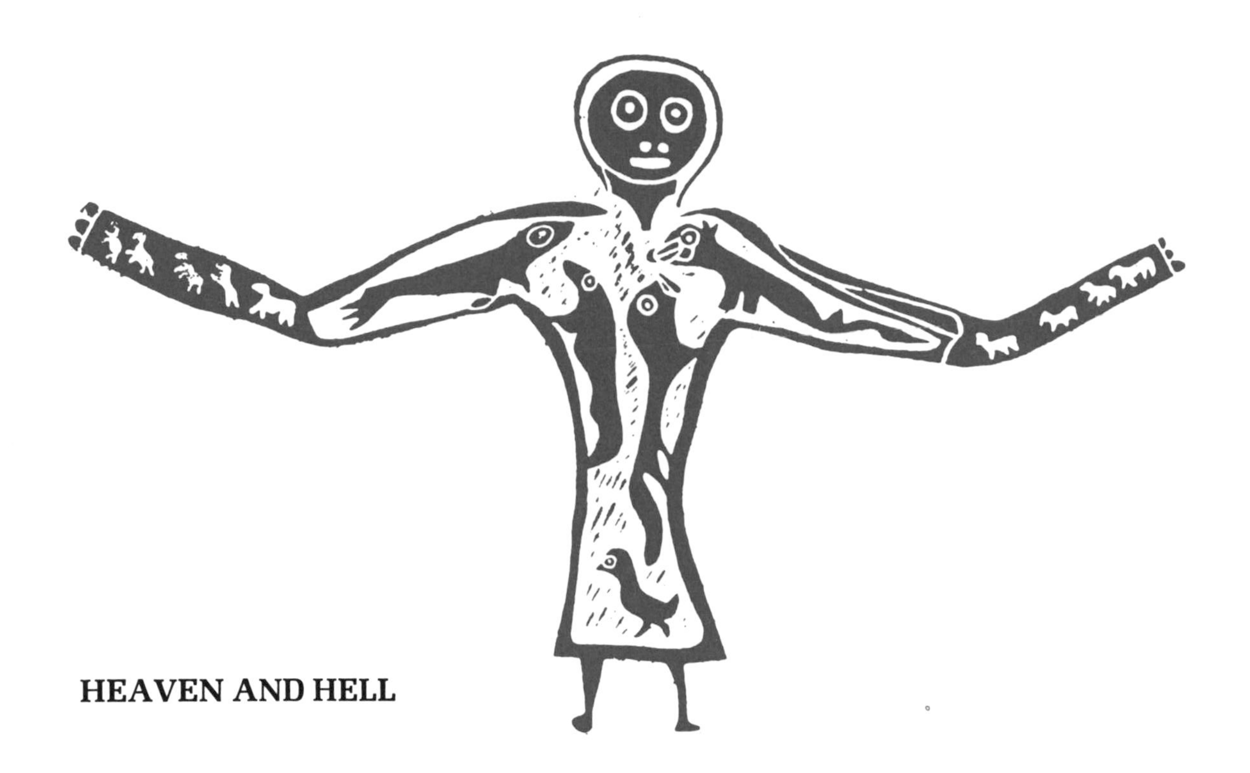

HEAVEN AND HELL

And when we die at last,
we really know very little about what happens then.
But people who dream
have often seen the dead appear to them
just as they were in life.
Therefore we believe life does not end here on earth.

We have heard of three places where men go after death:
There is the Land of the Sky, a good place
where there is no sorrow and fear.
There have been wise men who went there
and came back to tell us about it:
They saw people playing ball, happy people
who did nothing but laugh and amuse themselves.
What we see from down here in the form of stars
are the lighted windows of the villages of the dead
in the Land of the Sky.

Then there are two other worlds of the dead underground:
Way down deep is a place just like here on earth
except on earth you starve
and down there they live in plenty.
The caribou graze in great herds
and there are endless plains
with juicy berries that are nice to eat.
Down there too, everything
is happiness and fun for the dead.

But there is another place, the Land of the Miserable,
right under the surface of the earth we walk on.
There go all the lazy men who were poor hunters,
and all women who refused to be tattooed,
not caring to suffer a little to become beautiful.
They had no life in them when they lived
so now after death they must squat on their haunches
with hanging heads, bad-tempered and silent,
and live in hunger and idleness
because they wasted their lives.
Only when a butterfly comes flying by
do they lift their heads
(as young birds open pink mouths uselessly after a gnat)
and when they snap at it, a puff of dust
comes out of their dry throats.

Of course it may be
that all I have been telling you is wrong
for you cannot be certain about what you cannot see.
But these are the stories that our people tell.

TRANSLATOR'S NOTE

I did not translate these poems from the Eskimo language, but from the literal English renderings in the official records of Rasmussen's voyages published by the Royal Danish Archives. Rasmussen wrote down everything just as the Netsilik Eskimos told it to him. Therefore, I also had to translate the material from spoken to written words. When you talk you tell a lot by gestures, facial expressions, and the way you use your voice. And of course all that gets lost if you just copy down the words directly. I tried to put all that life back in, so that the reader would sense a real person in the words, in this case an Eskimo person with his earthy humor and warmth. There are no people more delightful.

I would like to thank Paul Schmidt of the University of Texas who originally suggested this project to me when he was working for Educational Services, Inc. (now Educational Development Corp.), as part of an experimental teaching program. I'd also like to thank Peter Dow and Barbara Herzstein of EDC and all the others there, too many to mention, who helped and encouraged me.

Edward Field

THE ARTISTS

KIAKSHUK,

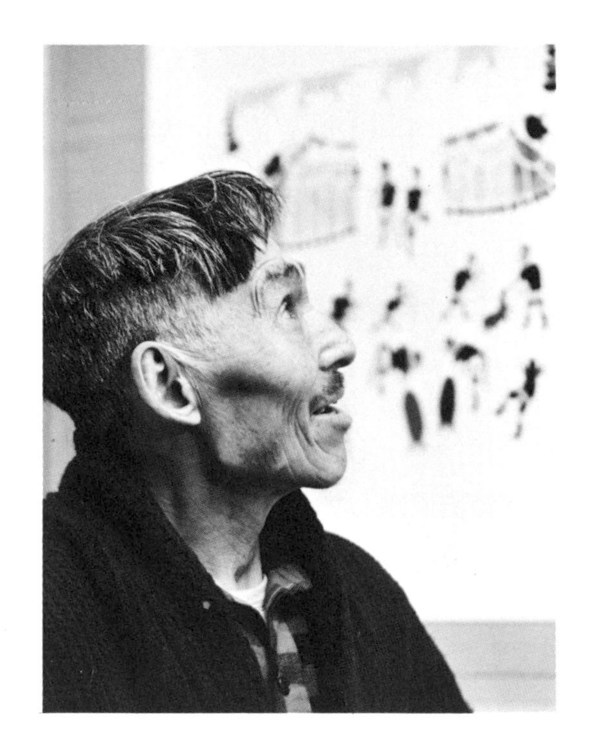

admired by many as one of the greatest Eskimo artists, died in 1966, nearly eighty years old. He was renowned among his people as a hunter, a storyteller, and a singer of the old songs. Kiakshuk was also rumored to have been a shaman (a kind of sorcerer, feared and admired for his supernatural powers). Although he was an old man when he began to draw, he produced a great many beautiful pictures, portraying all aspects of Eskimo life, hunting, fishing, and the world of the spirits. His son Lukta is also an artist as was his daughter Paunnichea who died in the the late sixties. Lukta is one of four artists entrusted with transferring the designs of the Cape Dorset printmakers to stone, including many in this collection.

PUDLO

is one of the most original of the Eskimo artists. For many years he lived almost alone in a remote camp near Amadjuak, the site of an abandoned Hudson's Bay Company post. In Pudlo's dramatic stencils and stone cuts, the world of the spirits, the magic which links the hunter and his prey, is given powerful expression. His wife Innukjuajuk, who died in 1972, was also an artist.

WEST BAFFIN ESKIMO COOPERATIVE

Pudlo is a member of the Eskimo community at Cape Dorset on West Baffin Island, as was Kiakshuk. The people of Cape Dorset have a long tradition of carving and craftsmanship. In the late 1950's, James Houston, an artist and Canadian government officer, encouraged the local artists to develop printmaking techniques. With the backing of the Department of Indian Affairs and Northern Development, a self-supporting cooperative known as the West Baffin Eskimo Cooperative was formed. The beautiful graphic art produced by the artists in this remote community just south of the Arctic circle is now exhibited and and admired throughout the world.

The signatures on each print identify the artist (top square), the printmaker (middle square), and the community (small igloo shape at the bottom, representing Cape Dorset).

SUGGESTED READING

Carpenter, Edmund S., ed. The Story of Comock the Eskimo. New York: Simon and Schuster, 1968.

Carpenter, Edmund S.; Varley, Frederick; and Flaherty, Robert. Eskimo. Toronto: University of Toronto Press, 1959.

Eber, Dorothy, ed. Pitseolak: Pictures Out of My Life. Seattle: University of Washington Press, 1972.

Freuchen, Peter. The Book of the Eskimo. Cleveland: World Publishing Co., 1961. Available in paperback.

———. I Sailed with Rasmussen. New York: Viking Press, 1958. Available in paperback.

Mary-Rousseliere, Guy; and Rasmussen, Knud. Beyond the High Hills. Cleveland: World Publishing Company, 1961.

Rasmussen, Knud. Across Arctic America. New York: G. P. Putnam's Sons, 1927.